LYNN REISER
THE SURPRISE FAMILY

GREENWILLOW BOOKS, NEW YORK

**THE ENDPAPER DESIGN IS ADAPTED
FROM THE AMERICAN QUILT PATTERN
"HEN AND CHICKENS."**

Watercolor paints and a black pen were
used for the full-color art.
The text type is Helvetica Light.

Greenwillow Books, a division of
William Morrow & Company, Inc.,
1350 Avenue of the Americas,
New York, NY 10019.
Printed in Hong Kong by South China
Printing Company (1988) Ltd.
First Edition
10 9 8 7 6 5 4 3 2 1

Library of Congress
Cataloging-in-Publication Data

Reiser, Lynn.
The surprise family / by Lynn Reiser.
   p. cm.
Summary: A baby chicken accepts a
young boy as her mother and later
becomes a surrogate mother for some
ducklings that she has hatched.
ISBN 0-688-11671-X (trade).
ISBN 0-688-11672-8 (lib. bdg.)
1. Chickens—Juvenile fiction.
2. Ducks—Juvenile fiction.
[1. Chickens—Fiction.
2. Ducks—Fiction.]
I. Title. PZ10.3.R293Su
1994   [E]—dc20
93-16249   CIP   AC

FOR
WARD
AND
JOHN WARD
AND
WARD AND JOHN

AND
PEEP—
HER STORY

First there was an egg.

One day it cracked open.

A baby chick looked out.
Nobody was there.

Where was her mother?

The baby chick looked up and saw—

a boy.

Her mother was a boy!
The boy was not the kind of mother
the chick had expected,
but she loved him anyway.

She followed him everywhere.
The boy showed
his baby chick
how to find
water and food
and grit
for her gizzard.

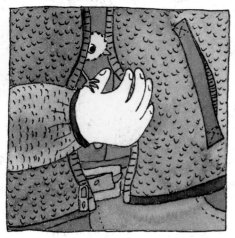

He taught her how to hide
safe inside his jacket
when a hawk flew by
or when the vacuum cleaner
came too close.

Every afternoon
the boy
and his baby chick
went for a walk
around the garden.

At night
she slept warm
under the edge
of his quilt.

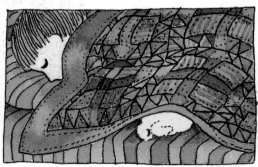

The baby chick grew and grew
and became a little hen.

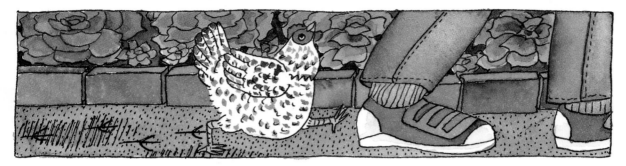

She still followed the boy everywhere,

but now following the boy was not enough.

She wanted a family to follow her.

She built a nest.

The boy found a clutch of eggs.

He gave them to the little hen.

She sat

and warmed the eggs,

and every day she turned the eggs,

and she sat

and she sat

and she sat

and she sat

and she sat—

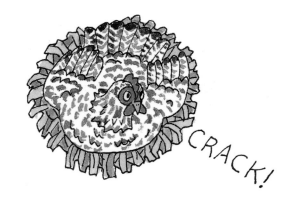

CRACK!

The eggs cracked open.

The babies looked out
and saw the little hen.

They followed her everywhere.
She showed them how to find
water and food

and grit
for their gizzards.

She taught them to run to her
when she sang a danger song
and danced a danger dance

and to hide

safe under her feathers.

Every afternoon the boy
and the little hen and the babies
went for a walk around the garden.

At night the babies slept

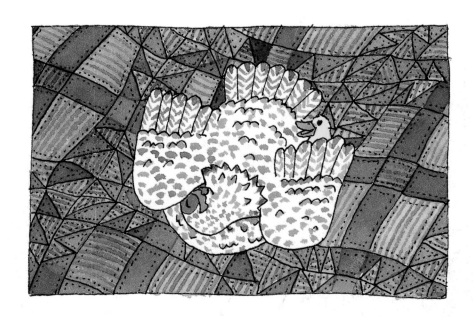

warm under the little hen's wings.

The little hen's family grew.
They still followed her everywhere,
but now walking around the garden
was not enough.
They wanted to walk by the pond.

So the boy
and the hen
took them to walk
by the pond.

They stood at the edge of the water.

They looked at the water.

They took a drink of the water.

They jumped into the water!

The little hen cried her DANGER cry—
her babies splashed.

The little hen danced her DANGER dance—
her babies swam.
The little hen held out her wings
for her babies to run under—

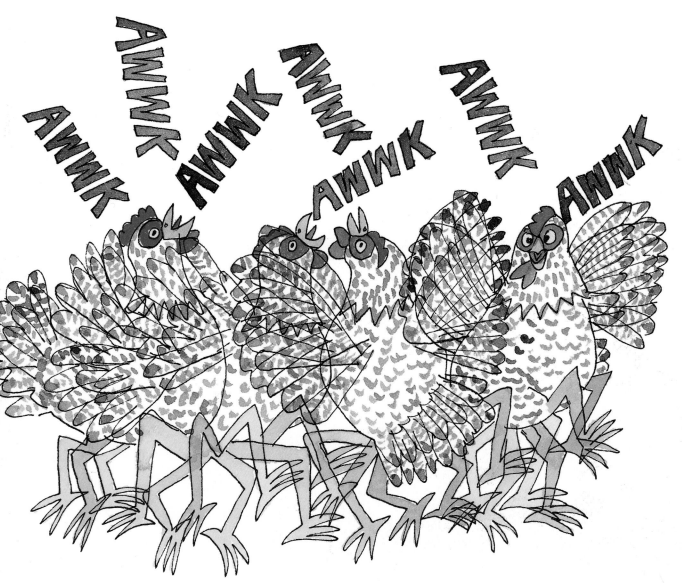

but they kept on swimming
farther and farther away.

The little hen ran after them,
but when her feet got wet,
she stopped.
She was a chicken.
Chickens cannot swim.

The little hen's babies
swam out of sight.

Only her boy was left.

Then the little hen's babies
turned around,

swam back,

hopped out of the water,

flapped their wings,

shook their tails,

and ran to their mother hen.

She gathered her babies in,
warm under her wings.
She looked at them.
They were safe.

She looked at them
again.
Carefully.

Their beaks were not pointed
like her beak,
or soft
like her boy's mouth—
they were flat.

Their feet were not sharp
like her feet,
or hard
like her boy's shoes—
they were webbed.

Their feathers were not fluffy
like her feathers,
or fuzzy
like her boy's jacket—
they were waterproof.

Her babies did not look like chicks
or like boys.
They looked like ducklings.

Ducklings were not the kind of family
she had expected,

but she loved them anyway.

The ducklings grew and grew
and became big ducks.
Some afternoons
while the ducks
swam in the pond,
the boy
walked around the garden,
and the hen followed him.
Some afternoons
while the ducks
swam in the pond,
the hen
walked around the garden,
and the boy followed her.
Other afternoons
while the ducks
swam in the pond,
and the boy waded after them,
the hen watched.

But every afternoon
in the garden
beside the pond,
after walking and swimming and wading,
there they all were,
together,
under the little hen's wings.

QUACK

MAY 1995